The MONSTER WHO LOST HiS MeaN

This book is dedicated to the
most beautiful M in the world.
I love you, Mom!
Thank you for everything.

—T. S. H.

To my cuddly monster,
Jonathan

—K. E.

ISBN 978-0-545-64300-9

Text copyright © 2012 by Tiffany Strelitz Haber.
Illustrations copyright © 2012 by Kirstie Edmunds.
All rights reserved. Published by Scholastic Inc.,
557 Broadway, New York, NY 10012, by arrangement with
Henry Holt and Company, LLC. SCHOLASTIC and associated logos are trademarks
and/or registered trademarks of Scholastic Inc.

12 11 10 9 8 7 6 5 4 3 2 1   13 14 15 16 17 18/0

Printed in the U.S.A.   40

This edition first printing, October 2013

The illustrations for this book were created digitally.

The MONSTER WHO LOST HiS MeaN

Tiffany Strelitz Haber

illustrated by

Kirstie Edmunds

SCHOLASTIC INC.

Monsters are a spooky bunch—
a scary, hairy group.
They run in packs, leave giant tracks,
and dine on eyeball soup.

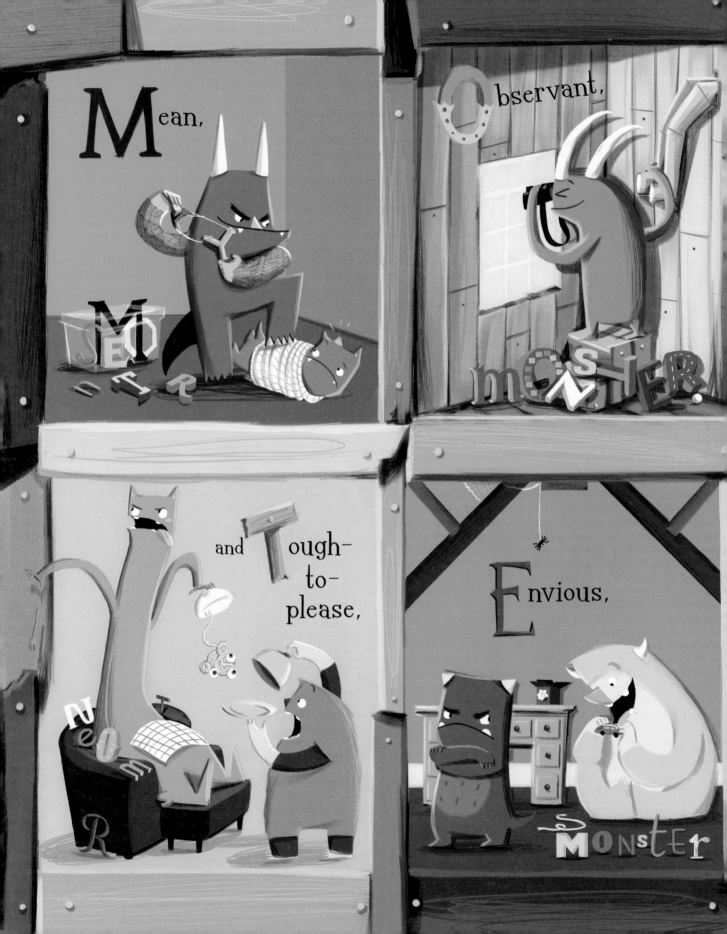

Noisy,

super Strong,

M**O**nster

Remarkable:

A **M**o**n**ster's ALL of these!

One day, a monster's M went missing,
gone without a trace!

And every M is custom-made,
the kind you can't replace.

So now he's just "The Onster,"
and the teasing never ends.
Not only has he lost his Mean—
he's lost his monster friends.

BOOM BOOM!
CRUNCH CRUNCH!

The Onster sits alone for lunch.

The Onster's sad
and starts to cry.

"I'm nothing since I lost my Mean!"
he sobs into his stew.
"I've got to find that M, or else
it's bye-bye, monster crew!"

The Onster tears through all his sheets

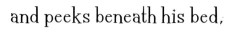
and peeks beneath his bed,

explores around the playground

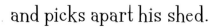
and picks apart his shed.

He empties every garbage can
in all of Monsterwood.

He even checks the engine
under every monster's hood.

He hangs his hairy head.

"Without my M, I'm not myself—
I'm someone else instead."

He can't be mean to human kids,
so why not help with chores?

Sweeping, heaping, light housekeeping,

organizing drawers.

He joins in all their soccer games
and rules at basketball.

He doesn't seem to miss
that missing 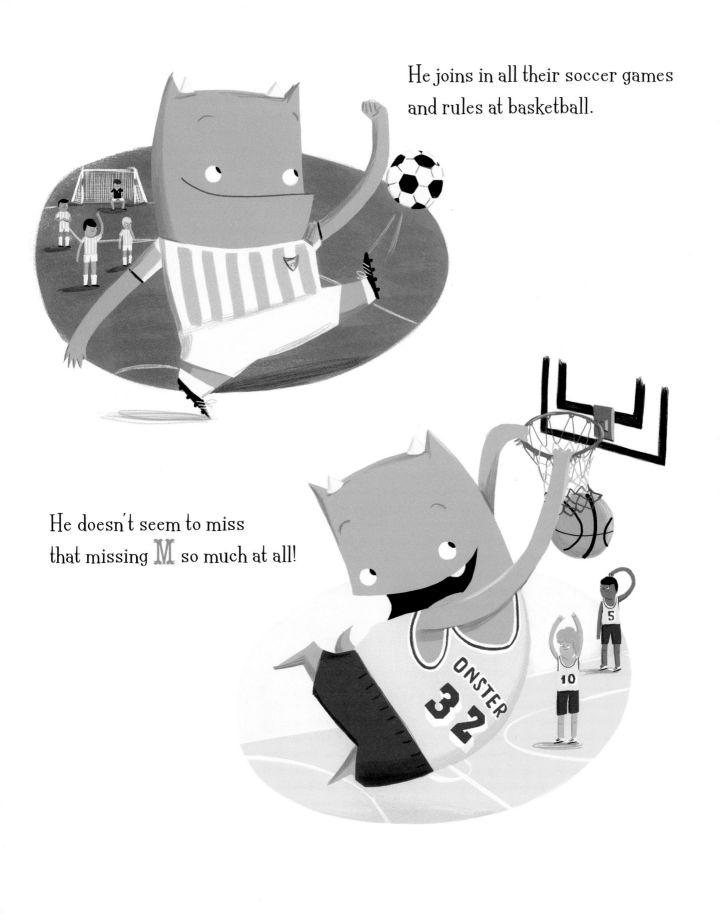 so much at all!

"I'm having tons of fun!" he laughs,
returning from a swim.
But then he hears some other monsters
making fun of him.

The Onster feels embarrassed—
he sees their point of view.
"I really need to stop this stuff
and do what MONSTERS do."

"Maybe I'll pretend I'm mean.
I bet it's not that hard.

Perhaps I'll pull the **FLOWERS**
out of Mrs. Power's yard!"

He stares at all the roses
in their stunning shade of red,
but just can't bear to harm them,
so he waters them instead.

The Onster thinks,

I'll throw some **EGGS** at Mr. Lander's van!

But winds up cooking brunch
for the entire Lander clan.

"I'm way too nice without my M—
my monster days are through.
I just don't fit in Monsterwood.
I'm not sure what to do."

He sadly heads on home again
with teardrops in his eyes.
He swings his front door open
and is greeted with . . .

A party in his honor!
The Onster's eyes grow wide.
His name and picture cover every
empty space inside.

I'm not a monster after all,
the Onster comprehends.
I may have lost my M, but then
I found amazing friends!

BOOM BOOM! POW POW!

The Onster waves and takes a bow.

LET'S HAVE THREE CHEERS!

HIP HIP HOORAY...

He's happier in every way!

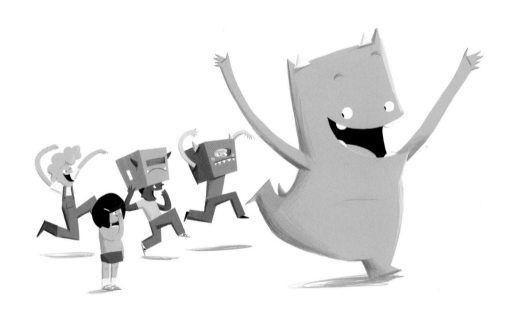